Original title
Published by Free Muske

Perspective

Christian Roos

America Star Books

First printing

Softcover 9781633825116
PUBLISHED BY AMERICA STAR BOOKS, LLLP
www.americastarbooks.com

The best way to see in future's perspective is to create the perspective itself.

THE ISOLATION

Today I'm going out to write. Maybe a little; maybe a lot, but I will write. The weekend has been good. I have been to many places and have seen many people. It felt beautiful.

But today, I choose isolation. Today, I will join and leave the world for what it is.

I leave for the big city. If I find myself in a big crowd, I probably wouldn't talk to anyone. I would say thank you when I get my sandwich or drink at the store, and that's it. I walk in the library and take a seat at the table where I've been for so many times. There are many people in this city, but there are still quiet places like the library. The atmosphere in this place turns my creativity on.

I never come here to rest. Throughout the week, I gathered the ideas that came to my mind. They were always somehow disorganized. All of those ideas take shape in all the letters that I write on paper. Sometimes, I leave it as it is and just read a book. After reading a few pages, I get back to writing. I kind of sentence myself to a temporary stay in this building. Every idea that I collect throughout the whole week, comes to life in this very place.

Sometimes the result is not how I wanted it to be. When that happens, I do some adjustments or just get back to it when I think it's time to do so.

And so another day passes. I am one step closer to the completion of a new book. Today I walk out satisfied. I'm ready to take what life has to offer.

HAUNT

If you look around you see ghosts. In the texts that are directed to you. In the words that are spoken with the best intentions to make you feel better. You do not see them. You just don't.

In the faces of people, you see ghosts. When one looks at you with a reassuring look, all is well. You don't worry. But if they just look away, you will see those ghosts appear. They whisper your distrust.

When you're alone, you think about ghosts. They fill the silence and you give them space to fill your thoughts. It's a duel between you and the imaginary beings. And again, you're on the losing side.

Everything has its origin. The ghosts had always been there. Fed, pampered and given the freedom to control you; when, where and how they want to. Has there been anyone who has actually said that ghosts do not exist?

Ghosts are not where you live. Not in your closet or under your bed.

They do not stand behind the door or the window. They do not hide themselves. It's only your self-destructive thoughts that project that kind of ghosts. You're the only spectator of what is projected on the large screen.

DUE MODESTY

I've always been interested about the stars and the planets. I've always been amazed at the universe and where everything is located. I've spent a lot of hours in the library and have carefully listened to all the lectures in school that had anything to do with it. When someone asked about a planet or a spaceship, I was always willing to tell them about it. There was just so much to share and we're sometimes never aware of any of it because we're too busy with the issues of our everyday lives. Somewhere out there, far above our heads, were beautiful spectacles like the Orion, the asteroid belt, Magellanic Clouds, and the comets.

As I got older, I went against the things I read. I rebelled against the things that I hear from everyone else about how men were created in the image of God. About how the universe was created by a creator, and that was how He had shown his greatness. The Bible, unfortunately, did not give me the answers to my questions. It was not a comforting thought that the earth was only created in six days when in reality, no object in our universe was created in only six days. The holy books were caught in different areas of science. The knowledge that came from the church doesn't last longer than what we really know about the universe. The earth is not the center of the universe and the sun does not revolve around the earth. The perspective of who we are is subject to change during the search for our place in the universe. And I think we will never completely understand the universe for it is too big and too complex.

The theories that I learned from other books, were to me, more beautiful than the texts from Genesis because they showed me that there is more than I had ever imagined. There is so much more to discover about the universe. If I've been looking for divinity, then the universe is the place to find it. The best approach we can take is to wonder with humility. We can only do justice to what we see by continuing to expand the knowledge we have about the universe. I drift more and more away from the people who say it has been a god who has it all figured out and created it. Science adjusts itself continuously to answer the unanswered previous questions. And so we are getting a little closer to the truth, to thereby conclude that the real and full truth will never reveal itself to us.

AFTER DEATH

I was surprised when you asked me what I thought about life after death. Usually you keep these thoughts to yourself. Because I did not see it coming, I had to think about it.

What I said after a brief silence was living in each individual soul. That is what remains after death. The soul will have found peace when you are free of feelings and struggles along your life. Free of hatred, resentment, and shame. Free from anger, envy, and jealousy. Those feelings block our freedom to live even after death. Once you are able to get rid of all those stuff, you can finally rest in peace.

You asked what happens after that. I did not know. I did not know what I believe in; judgment, hellfire, pearly gates and harps. The only peace that you experience is when you're in a deep sleep at night. That's heaven. Free from the worries of everyday life.

It's hell to live. There seems to be no end to it then you just get tired. Thus, it seems to me, if you are burdened with emotions that you cannot get over with, you can never really rest, even after death.

I could tell you how to get over them. It will be difficult if you grew up with a traditional Christian faith. You believe in the crucifixion, the resurrection, the second coming and the final judgment. I was reminded of the song by Stef Bos. We come back together after death? I think so. We both believe, after all, in heaven. Only in your perception, the sky look different.

The latter, I did not I tell you. I felt that that was enough substance to think about. Hopefully, death wouldn't be here anytime soon.

LASAGNA

I did not count them. I should do it. Occasionally, I joke about the number of dates I've had over the years. There has been a lot.

I have met most of them through the internet. I can still remember my very first internet date. It was on a December evening. I do not know how long we have been chatting or emailing. I think it has been for several weeks. She wrote at one point that she actually wanted to meet me. I thought it was a great idea because I had become quite curious about her. To her surprise, I suggested to see each other the following night. We both agreed.

The next night, I parked my car near the rendezvous point. I remember what I was thinking. I was really nervous. Who knows what would happen. Maybe whom I was going to meet is nowhere near the person whom I knew from the pictures. Maybe she isn't really nice but what did I have to lose? I was already there and the worst thing that could happen was me, not being there.

Then there she stood at the right and at the right place. I walked up to her and introduced myself (something I would regularly do with other women later on).

She seemed a little surprised when I gave her three kisses. We walked to a restaurant. I think it was an Italian restaurant. I remember I ordered lasagna. I also remember that I wasn't able to finish it. It wasn't that I don't like lasagna. It wasn't even the amount of cheese. I was just head over heels in love at that time.

The talks went smoothly; about work, family, friends, and about faith. We had a drink at a nearby pub. We continued talking. We talked about being happy, about love, health, and going out.

I offered to take her home. No, not because I wanted something more to happen but it was just out of courtesy.

"That would be nice." she said.

When I got home, I received a text message. I can't remember the precise text. Whether it was about wanting to see me again, I do not know. But a week later, we met again. We went to town and had another nice evening. The best was yet to come. Just before she left, she asked me about our situation. It was a very bold and honest move for a woman who was still fairly inexperienced with romance. I told her that I thought she was totally awesome. That made her very happy and she gently kissed me.

What followed was a stormy relationship that unfortunately did not last long. It made me go back to the Internet. I went to many dates. Some are worth describing while others are not. Since it is not proper to not finish your food, I've never ordered lasagna with cheese on a first date.

BACHELOR

The house is dark. All the time that I've been away, nothing has changed. My stuff are still in the same place and the plants have not been watered yet.

I turned a few lights on. The glass on the counter suggests that last night was a lot of fun. I did not want to wash it so I could use it so I just grabbed another glass from the cupboard. The vessel is much larger than the other glasses. The pans on the stove irritated me because they still weren't clean.

So I'm back home after I've been away for a long time. It has been a pleasant evening without confusing happenings such as unintended sex.

At this point in my life, I want to have everything. I do what I want. How I want it. When I want it. Nobody gets to tell me what to do. I have arranged my life on my own taste. But still, the house is quiet. And for a moment, I feel alone.

I realize what needs to happen. I am, in a sense, happy on my own. This has been going on for far too long. I feel like a traitor to myself. I am a sociable person. I have a lot to give to others. I would be a good husband and a nice father. It will be a waste if I don't become one. Next week, I might wake up next to a stranger again, but that does not change anything; another woman, the same emptiness, and meaningless flings.

I turn out the lights. The house was dark again. There is not a word spoken. I'm single, but I don't really feel free. I know I can be more than this.

FLOOR

There was a time when we were boys. Men often act like boys. We talk about things that we always do; football, girls, and cars.

We shared what we wanted and could share. We don't really share our deeper feelings. It's good that way. Life had so much in store of us. Later, when we have been tried and tested, and worn out by years, we would be sitting with each other and then say the things that we have always had in our minds that were never spoken out loud.

We were simply satisfied with who we were. We even bought *Playboy* at the store just to look at it. That's what men do.

Much later when were no longer boys, we looked back on decades of friendship. And there was the floor. The hand of time had touched us. I told you I was proud of you; about what you had achieved without any envy. You have kids, a lovely wife. A family to care for. For me, those are the most beautiful things in the life of a person.

On your turn, you told me you were proud of all the years of our friendship. Sincerity and warmth, caught in a moment. Years ago, it seemed almost unthinkable to exchange kind words like this. We got this far and that's the advantage of getting old and becoming wiser.

We are able to look back; to estimate the value of things. These are moments that are golden. I value this kind of conversations. We have grown and ended up having this moment.

WADI RUM THOUGHTS

Sitting on a rock in the Wadi Rum desert in Jordan, I watch the sunset and listen to the complete silence. It's that kind of moment where we find complete silence. Silence around us. Silence in your heart. Pure silence that makes you listen to the voice within. The voice is drowned out by the hustle and bustle of your everyday life like to run and not to have to come late. We usually have no time to sit down and listen to what our conscience has to say. Silence is, for some people, makes them a little anxious. They feel like something must be said; that there must be sound. Without it, we are left alone with ourselves and thrown back to the voice in our hearts; for a confrontation or a revelation. For me, at this time, it's the latter. Finally, with just myself, the voice in my heart had a lot to say.

I listened intently. How my heart had missed me. I have had so little time for him. I was always at work, never even acknowledged my deep feelings that my heart carries. At that time, I made the appointment with my heart more often to listen to him. Once a day, I close my eyes and be quiet so I could just feel; melancholy feelings, really. To be able to sit alone without being lonely without the attention.

CHANGE THE WORLD

When I was walking on the street many years ago, I had only one goal. I walked as fast as I could. I stepped off the train with confidence and walked into the crowd. Normally, I don't enjoy being around large groups of people but this time, it didn't bother me because I have that goal in mind. It was to see you again. I was no longer a teenager so I felt confident.

Actually, I had always liked to see you. Sometimes, when we do not see each other for a while, you disappear from my mind. Then I saw you again, and began to carefully feel the butterflies flatter in my stomach. It's hard to say why I've never done anything about those butterflies. I only looked for something that would reflect my feelings; like songs. There is a song by Eric Clapton called *Change the world*.

"If I could change the world,
I would be the sunlight in your universe. "

He sang what I thought about you.

As always, you looked happy and cheerful. You told me about your new found love. I slowly felt the blood drain from my face. I think I felt very cold for a while. Everything you told me from the fifteen minutes just went from one ear to the other. I started to think if you noticed it; that I felt lost.

I told myself to stop whining about it. I didn't take the chance while I had it and thought that it was too little to late. I decided to act like a real man and just tried to make it a nice day with you. It was a nice day but I still kept thinking about the what ifs. What if we always spent days like this more often? What if?

On the way home I thought about that song again. The song that always reminded me of you. *Change the world.*

And I knew for sure that if I could, I would change the world.

"You would think my love was really something good."

I really would have done it. I would have started with you and me. Eric Clapton understood what I really felt.

A SPECIAL CHRISTMAS CARD

Most cards have one or more names on the inside. Some of them already have printed messages but sometimes, some people still take the time to write a short personal text on it.

There's one particular Christmas card that I will always remember. It was from the parents of a girlfriend that I had.

I visited them a few days before Christmas. Her life wasn't easy. Hospitalizations, problematic relationships, and mentally draining situations. We only see each other a few times a year but we both know that we're always there for each other.

The text written on the card hit me immediately. "We are pleased with your friendship. You mean a lot to her." I asked myself whether this is the most of what I can achieve as a human being.

There are so many things that I could be, right? I know that others know that too.

I do not know if people are destined to do certain things in life and not other things. I'm not sure yet. I do not know if this is my destiny. But if this is my job for the rest of my life, I wouldn't mind. It feels good to be valued by others. I would almost say that nothing compares to that feeling but I'm sure I'm still going to experience more beautiful moments. That moment was a pretty picture in my rich picture book. That Christmas card is one of the many.

BODY

Your body already spoke volumes when you opened the door. Before I could get in, I had to get through you first. You never step aside before you got what you wanted. Three kisses from me, and you got them. Also, the fact that you sat down on the two-seater, next to me meant to me something. Namely, that you were glad I was there. Even though there were enough seats in the room, you sat next to me. But the space between us was still about fifteen inches. As the evening progressed, the space was getting smaller. The attraction was obvious, and after half an hour, I hit my arm on the back of the sofa and felt the tips of your hair.

Very shortly after you put your hand on my knee, you quickly take it away. That is body language. Meanwhile, I was busy trying to translate everything. If I understood it right, you wanted more than just chatting. The next step was an obvious but not less exciting. My right knee softly kissed your left thigh. You allowed it.

I moved in a little closer and my fingertips were now on your shoulder. My other hand left the couch and began to explore.

The sensation poured through my body. It could happen any time now. If we would keep looking at each other long enough, our lips would also make an active contribution to this evening (apart from talking and drinking red wine).

And then it happened. We held each other's gaze a bit longer than the average three seconds. We were like two magnets that could not escape from each other. A first tentative kiss and then another, and another one. Our hands soon explored each other's bodies. What all seemed inevitable all evening, had already started. Suddenly you stood resolutely and said with a serious look on your face, "I'm going to the bathroom, then you may give me the massage you promised." Your body language was obvious and exciting.

Not much more than that

It's everyone for themselves and each other. That was pretty much the best thing he could give. But much better than what he had to say, she would have never heard. He was convinced. "Look," he said. "We can point fingers at other people trying to convince their mistakes. But that will be pointless."

Moments earlier, she had come up to him to talk about serious issues such as world peace, the hardening of the society and the individualization of society. He always had an opinion about everything, and she was eager to learn and was only too happy to listen to wise counsel.

"As long as we continue to talk about what other people should do, it will not change anything.

To make it easy to say: we all have a light in us, and that should be contagious to others. So he again finds himself in the light that shines on other people.

"That is all we can do."

She was not convinced that it was so simple. Because if it is so easy, why is peace so far? "You're thinking too hard. Humanity looks for answers that are so easy to find. Do not do to another what you would not like others to do unto you. Speak no evil against someone else. Help the fateful: the stranger, the enemy. Through those things, you will be a light for everyone. "

She had not really thought of that. She realized that she could not do more than that. And if everyone does that, then…

But maybe that's too hard to imagine. It's every man for himself these days. The most socially-selfish thought exists. And all he could do was to convey his wisdom to others. Share the light by giving the candle to the other. For two people can me a difference. Though it appears little to the outside world.****

MORE THAN A THOUSAND STARS

It was one of those nights when we made efforts to understand each other. We were in the same room but we were emotionally miles apart. You, swimming in your emotions, and I, persevering.

We decided to go back to the place that became a symbol of disagreement for the last few hours. It was dark and cold outside. We were quiet for a while until you looked up. You looked at the dark blanket that had stretched over us you always have wondered what was out there.

"Sometimes, you're just like the heaven." you said. "Misunderstood and versatile. I already know you for a while, but I still do not feel like I really know you. Like the stars in the sky that are sometimes difficult to see but if you do, it looks lovely. It's like you're a mosaic of a thousand hues. Maybe that's why I've fallen for you. "

"Perhaps you're right," I said. "I am indeed not an ordinary person, but if you give me time, I'll show you how valuable I can be for you. You compare me as a group of more than a thousand stars. But you're right; stars sparkle and what's the use of those lights if I'm not going to share them?" I could see how the moisture in your eyes reflected the moonlight. How beautiful it is when sincerity and honesty can bring people closer together. Gone was the distance. Gone was the misunderstanding. We were back as a whole. More than a thousand stars were, that evening, our witnesses.

THE GOLD RIM

Several people have inspired me in my life, and you're one of them. The way you speak, the sobriety with which you stood in life, and the courage with which you handled things.

I was not much younger than you but you clearly had more life experience. What I experienced for the first time was a piece of cake for you. My first kiss was when you already had a lot of relationships behind. Each new challenge for me, you'd already seen.

And yet we seemed to be friends for life and we picked out the best together. Both of us were blessed with a good sense of humor and could laugh about the simplest things. But there was also room for serious, in-depth conversations. We've been chattering about everything that kept us busy. It was on top of a hill in Germany, during a sultry summer in August, when we talked about the chances of happiness in love, the prospects of having a good job, the importance of good health and the need for expressing our creativity.

It was a magical evening. We discussed everything that we have come in contact with in life. As we talked, we had a view of a valley below, and we saw the lights of small villages and cars. Above us, the stars looked silently down on us. Oddly enough, it was also a farewell moment. You found the love of your life that holiday and since then, our ways moved and were no longer parallel. Still, I think back about all those moments; the hours we wandered through the city, the many movies we watched together, and the moments at our school canteen. Everything was still clear in my mind.

Therefore, this is for you. You were one of the people in my life, who appeared and then disappeared again and again but it was all beautiful.

THE VELVET HAND

There is a lot to be proud of. There is a lot to be happy for. I remember when you asked me if I ever think in a different way. Or there are times if I see things in a not so positive way.

Those moments are definitely there. I also remember that I explained to you how it works for me.

It's like I got a built-in mechanism, which always brings me back to the right path. Everyone has moments of doubt, sadness or despair in his life. It's like when I'm barely hanging on, there's a velvet hand pushing me from the other side until I back in the light. There are certainly giving all sorts of explanations, but whatever it is, it works. And it has brought me to where I am now. I'm grateful for that.

The velvet hand has become a part of me. It gives me a push in the right direction if I don't know where to go.

"Go. Walk on. I'm with you. I'll be there when you waver."

It was to live well. And by living in a way that suits me, I can also be good for other people. Good for me is good for you and vice versa. No, life is not a constant flower and I do not bathe all day in the sunlight, but I do always find my way.

Your reaction was somewhat nonchalant, like you would not believe me. That day, you do not need the hand I offered you. The magnificent velvet of my hand did visibly hurt your eyes.

BEAUTIFUL IN THE MORNING

Waking up beside you is a good way to start my day. Your little eyes looking curiously around, then you stretch slowly.

The smile on your mouth betrays a zest of life that is inspiring, and I still think back to that day. I like how your hair is all tangled like the forest. You glow even without makeup on. I just want to keep you longer in my arms. You look so beautiful in the morning. You look pure, natural, and innocent.

We cuddle until it is time to face the day. We both go our way through the house then come back together at the table for breakfast. You have your patterns and I have mine. Sometimes we laugh about it, but we accept them and leave them the way they are.

You look nice after your morning routines. You look ready for the world out there, but I already miss what I saw earlier; the beauty that I get to witness every time I wake up beside you.

The time has come to go our separate ways. I look back at you one more time, and so do you. I kiss you once more. May this day be as beautiful as the morning that I just spent with you.

THE LAST POST

For a moment, they were chained in a truth that they both had in mind. They could clearly hear each other, but it was as if they had trouble to really understand each other. Both were determined to make the call go smoothly. On the television, the news anchor had started reading the news on political tensions and stubborn heads.

When one of the two realized that they were already silent for quite a while, one had decided to carefully break the ice. One had expressed regret over the way things had gone and told how it could be better for the next generation. The news on the television was now on to the next topic: the road map to peace in the Middle East. The word regret was a good move. The other said it was all not intended and that it had not, indeed, earned any good outcome but it could be a good lesson for next generation; that they might come out stronger.

For the first time during the call was laughter after one had expressed the obvious tension. They were both relieved that they had talked about it. They both understood that communicating is important as well as expressing their emotions to each other. He tried to explain that while he stared at the television screen.

In his imagination, came on the last news: Peace between two people in the Netherlands had been signed again. The news anchor wished everyone a good night. He turned off the television because he had nothing more to hear. For him, all was said and discussed.

A SOFT LANDING

It's been a long, hard day. I can barely think straight. There are one or several occasions throughout the day that I should have thought of myself more and I did not give in to the issues of the day.

"Of course I will."

"Yeah, I get that sometimes."

"I can do to it."

My spirit haunts my head and makes no attempt to stop. Various temptations await. E-mails are waiting to be answered, television programs want to be watched, and my phone wants attention.

I choose to ignore all of that. I don't think anything bad could happen if I just ignore them for a while. I turn the radio on. The classics station is playing Gabriel Faure's *Claude Monet*.

This is exactly what every fiber in my body asked for. The light in the room is muted and while I'm on the couch, I let the music kidnap my me. I start to relax. The rush is over. It's just me and the music. I start to feel my inner peace.

THE PROPHET

In the past recent years, I have been in different countries. The amount of scheduled flights you have, determines how big your world really is. You can see plenty of the world out there. How you view the world is just a matter of perspective. Airports give me a worldly sense, but that feeling does not compare with the worldly sense of a large bookstore or library. Thousands of books on a wide variety of topics are waiting to be discovered.

It was just another day when I stepped into the shop. Dozens of people shuffled past each other and sniffed the books. I got a feeling that I often get when I am there. I probably do not have enough life to be able to read everything that I want to. That's simply too much demand for a man.

I remember that I felt dispirited that day so I could use a mental boost. In the Department of *Philosophy*, I came across a book by the writer Kahlil Gibran. His book *The Prophet* is a well-known book and it was on my wish list. I decided to browse through the book. While I was reading, I decided that I might as well join the people who were sitting with their books. When I was halfway through, I thought I might as as well but the book so I did.

Oddly enough, the book did take my sad feeling that day. The love that I had for the book was pure and intense. It was a rainy day but it made me feel like the sun pushed through the clouds to shine on me. If the soul of that writer has a color, it was probably a bright and shiny hue. I read about love; about me;

about good and evil; about self-knowledge; about children. That man must have been a huge thinker. I was reading the feelings I have all this time. It was like standing at the edge of a pool and being hesitant to jump into the water that bore my reflection. It was like I was afraid to face my own feelings.

"The soul unfolds itself like the countless petals of a lotus." said Gibran. I have, that day, once again experienced my mind unfolding in a space where I can gain knowledge. So I love my world. So I build happiness. And there is not a plane anywhere in the world that will take you to it.

PASSION

I don't have a lot of interest about cycling, but when I hear some people talk about it, it arouses my curiosity. I thought it was only a lot of fun for the deprived ones. However, I think of them as people who only do it for convenience. They just want to do something to know that they are still there.

People's excitement is contagious. Years ago, a writer named Büch traveled around the world to look for traces of the yore civilization. I remember he had a book in his hand which was centuries old.

The man was as happy as a child with what he had found. It might be hard to imagine what's so special about it, but whether the book was interesting or not, he was still able get others interested about it. I like people who have a passion for something. They do what they do because they love it, and not because they want everyone else to follow.

A year or so ago, I once came home with a man who had decorated his house in an unconventional way. It was full of stuff, but it was not messy. Antique lamps, clocks, cameras, and photographs of several people looked at me. The man had a fondness for that kind of stuff so he collected them. It gave him peace and he told me that the ticking of many clocks didn't disturb him. It was his passion and because of it, his identity is formed.

When we follow our hearts, our true identity shows. Not so much for others but for ourselves. If we look in the mirror, we see ourselves clearer. The mirror then talk back, "Go for what you want and do not let anyone stop you. Discover and create your happiness. Nobody else does it for you. It's up to you." A lot of cyclists understand that.

I was at home when I hear that someone has climbed the Alpe d'Huez, with his own strength, perseverance and great passion. It might not been put on the television but I know that it was passion that brought him where he wanted to be.

THE SAMPLE

She stood there with her arms on her sides and looked sympathetically at him. It was the time to be concerned about the situation they have landed on. It seemed like a complicated situation and it was never ending. They talked about their shortcomings. He couldn't deny that he had always been against her and that he thought more about his own happiness than both of theirs. To say the least, he was very selfish.

"What have you been carrying all this time?" he asked her. She talked about the burden she carried with her. It just never goes away. She said that there are already a number of years when she had a monster chained to her back. There were times when she did not notice it was there but then it could suddenly make themselves be heard again and. She suspected that the sample does distort the truth sometimes. It whispers lies about other people. It says that some people she loves cannot be trusted. It outlines ghost stories in her head about what could happen between them. Or that she was never good enough. She said she didn't want to think that way but nothing will change as long as the sample does not leave her alone. She was sorry that she had to tell him about it but if he wanted them to work out, she needed him to defeat that monster.

"The biggest battle you have to carry is yourself." he said. "When you overcome the inner struggle, the monster will lose strength. It will, slowly but surely, slip away from you. Does the sample have a name? Did it say where it comes from?" he asked.

She said: "The sample originated and grown at times of my greatest uncertainty, when I started carrying it as a burden. The sample told me: "I am here because of you and my name is Jealousy."

THIS MAN

The feeling was there again. It was not the first time he experienced this kind of feeling. Once in a year, he would feel it and he knew too well what it meant.

This man was the one who brought him to where he was and he was satisfied with it. That was until that feeling had come back to him.

A few years ago, he had a dream but now, that dream seemed outdated and barely brought him satisfaction. The dream was realized but new dreams had presented themselves.

A few years ago, he had a goal but now, it seemed like an island that he had left behind. For quite some time, he was young and ambitious. There were so many things that he wanted to experience. This man wanted the solitary life and to leave that all behind. This man was to encounter the love of his life and decided it was time for the next step. Gone were the lonely nights. Gone were the dreams about what it would be like to share life with someone else. His life had changed dramatically and thus its objectives. The time had come to start sharing his life with the person he loved.

This man was living in a city that was once his place but he started to feel more and more of a stranger. He heard the calling sounds of the city where he came from. It was time to come home. This city had been good to him and he had many beautiful moments with it but it was not his city. He had the feeling that his future lay elsewhere. Every fiber in his body screamed for change and it had to be soon. This man was not made to sit where he was sitting. The story of this man was prosecuted because the feeling was there again, and the time had come to move on.

IT IS WHAT IT IS

It's hardly the first time that I walk around here. And you can call that an understatement. It is the sixth time this year. Some people find it strange. Others may admire or appreciate it. But it is absolutely true that I am a fan of the environment in which I am standing: the amusement park, Efteling in Kaatsheuvel. It's not that I have socio emotional behind my peers. I had a happy childhood and I am quite rational in life. In short, I'm sure there's nothing wrong with me; nothing more and nothing less. Some people sit every week in a football stadium. Other people sit weekly in the pub. Others still go into video games stores. It all has its value. I do not believe that it is necessary to look for the roots of my passion. Sometimes it is sometimes good to adapt things as they are. It is what it is.

And with that, I have described in a nutshell, why the park is such an attraction to me. It's just what it is. It is a place where I particularly enjoy and many may not understand.

Efteling symbolizes a world that I know. The stories that are hidden will, over a hundred years, still be told by people. It is what it is, and in a world of constant change, it is a very pleasant thought.

MOONWALK

I was seven years old. It was 1983 and it was the first time I'd seen him on the television. It was very historical for what I was about to see would have a great impact on my life. It was the first time I was going to experience to be really devoted to someone.

The man was standing in a light beam on the stage and took a pose. The fedora, glove and glitter socks were present. Those were his trademarks for so many years. His skinny body moved to the beat.

Seemingly effortless and completely at ease, he gave off a dazzling show. The audience was completely hysterical. It was the combination of those things that had me perplexed. Of course, the music always comes first, but the way he shared his music with the audience from that moment, made me an absolute fan. A little boy was completely enchanted by what he saw and heard. Every fiber in my body let me know that this was made for me. This was definitely my thing!

I was eleven years old. It was 1988. With a lot of smoke and screeching guitar music, he entered the stage. There he was at last. Five years after I saw him for the first time on television, he was in real life. He was a speck in the distance, but his voice was unmistakably his. Every word I sang along. I could not hide my excitement and went completely out of my mind. This was an evening not to be forgotten. Michael Jackson was in the Netherlands and I was there.

Years later, on my thirty-third birthday, my dad called early morning for two reasons. First of all, to greet me happy birthday and then second was to tell me that Michael Jackson was dead. I couldn't believe it. I sprinted to the television to see if it was on the news. What my father said was not a bad joke but just the sad reality. I spent that morning on the internet and played all his songs. I also watched a lot of his videos.

Despite all the scandals that have been there around him, I still trusted him. He has written too many songs that I find so incredibly good and achieved so much that made me believe that if you really want something, everything is possible. He has been the living proof. If you want something, you can achieve it.

I still think back to that time in 1983. The beam has been extinguished. The stage is empty but the memories remain and his music is always around me.

THE FOOTBALL COACH

He sounded confident when he spoke to us. I had to believe him but I didn't know it at that time. What he told me didn't really sound absurd. He said that I had reached and had to cherish my age. I was fifteen years old and the best time of my life had come. He did not say that next year would be bad but he said that I had to enjoy what this year would bring. The guys from my football team were of the same age and we all listened carefully to what our coach had to say. Frankly, at the time it did not sound very logical in my ears. Being fifteen year old also had its drawbacks. Although I must admit that my life was doing pretty good. It was all very well organized.

I was in a fun class, did pretty well in school, and played every week. My game of football and girls were several reasons why it was nice. But I also had my worries. My grades and whether the girl was in love with me or not.

Looking back, I can conclude that our coach had the right to speak. There were relatively a few problems and when I gradually got older, life would be more complex. The more I got, the more I experienced. I learned that everything has its price. Life was good but the more you reach, the more you can lose. The man was quite right. I was fifteen, lived under the wings of my parents, and learned step by step to stand on my own.

Now, years later, I can say that one of my most carefree times was the year that I was fifteen. Everything was just simple during those days.

MAN DAY

In the train, on the way to Utrecht, I pass stations that are known to me. I have this route I often traveled. I love Utrecht. The city symbolizes pleasure for me.

The coupe is filled. I'm alone. After the first station, A Muslim girl is sitting diagonally opposite me. She wears a headscarf and has beautiful brown eyes. So dark they are almost black. Sometimes I look at her. Usually they do not look back, but when they do, they almost look right through me. I'm struggling to not keep looking back. I wonder where she is going and what she will do there. I wonder if she was born in the Netherlands and if not, where.

I forget that I have a book with me but that is almost not interesting anymore. I look at her again. She sits with her hands folded.

We are approaching Station Woerden. I know because I know the route. And my object of study knows it too, perhaps because it is broadcasted on the train; maybe because she lives there. Who can say? Questions, questions, questions. How are people still interesting when they remain silent?

She stands up and walks towards the only exit. Other people come into the train. The coupe was fuller. The chair where the girl sat remained unoccupied for a moment. A married couple is sitting opposite me. They both look at me. They are sitting silently next to each other. The man hardly seems to be interested to his wife or girlfriend. He looks outside. His wife seems to look past him at the same point.

I wonder if they are happy together. After a few minutes, she starts talking about the tiles in the backyard that will come next week. He starts talking back and there, began a real conversation. For some reason, I feel glad.

The couple remains until we reach Utrecht CS. For them, it is the final destination. I know that I sometimes, get tired of people. They are always around me, and I often need to sit all by myself. But today, I enjoy people. With all their differences and their backgrounds, people become more than interesting to me. Thoughts take me anywhere when I quietly observe them. That's a nice past time when you sit in the train. I will meet old friends later. Today is the man day for me.

FAITHFULNESS

It's Sunday afternoon. We stand at the door and you say that you just checked your mailbox. You let me know you appreciate that I am able to visit you again and that I should come over for dinner again soon. You'll make meatballs, potatoes, and beans. I look forward to it. Everything is wonderfully familiar. You say that I'm always so loyal. Actually, I do not know any better. After all, how can I not be faithful?

You wave goodbye. You are just as loyal to me. You never fail. It's already dark so I promised to ring you so you'd know that I got back home safely.

On the way home, I thought about what you said. I am faithful. But dear grandmother, how can I have?

Faithful to you also means loyal to the people I love, and family is one of the most important things in life.

I think of the many moments that I spent at your home; from a little boy to an adult man. Every milestone in my life, you have witnessed. When I graduated, I moved, or a book that I wrote. You've seen it all.

Faithfulness means, to you, all those moments when I was with you. Being true means, to you, to be faithful to other people we have known, and there are now no more; my other grandfather and grandmothers. I realize that all these people are the basis of my roots. My origin. I take another look in my mirror and see your flat fading behind me. Faithful means, to you, to be faithful to my past. Being true means, to you, being faithful to myself.

NO HOPE

Her eyes were empty. Her voice was monotonous. There were a lot of people happy; their hope drawn from the events of recent days. But her hope was gone.

Despite the fact that her brother had become a symbol of resistance, he worked hard to provide for his family. He wanted to study but they had no money for it so every day, he was on the street with a cart full of fruits and vegetables. Not that he was complaining. He was a guy who always laughed and smiled. But unfortunately, laughter destroyed him.

One day, he was once harassed by a police officer. He would not be authorized to do what he did. He needed a license in Tunisia. He protested when his scales were also seized. He was brutally beaten by two male officers. As if that was not enough, his deceased father was insulted. Desperately, he tried to submit a complaint to the local authorities. No one listened to him.

With the little money he had, he bought gasoline and set himself on fire at the entrance of the government building. He died two weeks later in a hospital near Tunisia.

With the fire he has ignited is a chain reaction. Many people were hoping, after this man had no hope. Many people tasted freedom after this man's hope was lost. Meanwhile, the politicians were worried in the West. They were worried about the "stability" and economic growth in their place. But it was not the Islamists that unleashed the fire of the revolution. It was not the people with beards who took the streets to argue for an Islamic state. It was the common people whom had become sick of injustice and stood up for their freedom. Because the reality was that, the people had no voice. Meanwhile, the rulers enriched themselves at the expense of the people. In the eyes of the West, Tunisia was "stable" and economic ties were holier than human.

"Thanks to my brother, people in this country have got air again." the woman said. "But we almost suffocate. People on the street are crying tears of joy but ours will never dry. "

Despite the revolution, they had no hope. The price they had to pay for that was simply too high.

SUMMER RESIDENT

It is a summer evening and I cannot sleep. The heat has made itself master of the city. Almost all day, it's hot in my bedroom. The windows are open but that seem useless. I toss and turn but that doesn't help. I just can't get some sleep. I'm wide awake and a dog is barking out on the street. I hear its owner call it but it's not working. I decide to just read. The book is next to my bed and it's as if it's waiting for me because it knew I won't be able to sleep. The climax of the book is slowly leading me to its ending but I keep the denouement for tomorrow. Nothing is as fun as saving the excitement for later. It's like keeping the last bit of a chocolate. The knowledge that there is something fun waiting for you makes life so much better. Or even better when you've forgotten about the chocolate then you suddenly remember it. I got out of my bed to watch some television. Not much was on. The only ones that fascinate me were the news replay and a couple of trailers for programs that are to come soon. I went back to bed and tried to get some sleep again.

I think about what I've seen on television. The news made me see demonstrations around the world. Brazil, Egypt, China... people revolt against the policies of their government. Oh yeah, tomorrow is incidentally oppressively hot again, the weatherman predicted. The news was followed by an announcement of the program "Summer Guests". Every year, there is a lot of attention to who the guests are. It's just an interview program. Why is that so special? I promise myself the answer to the question I have. Meanwhile, I picture me as one of the guests who sits on the chair. The thought makes me smile a little. Why would a simple man fill three hours of the program? But ridiculous or not, the thought continues. I give my opinion about the political climate in the Netherland that will lead me to the political system: the coalition. In that way, the leftmost and rightmost parties can now work together, while in the campaign, their beliefs are different as day and night. The PVV are going to pay. Geert Wilders probably does not know the word nuance. The Netherlands in recent decades has been too tolerant towards immigrants.

But there is also room for positivity. Beautiful music comes over. I say that Johnny Cash' *For the good times is* one of the most beautiful renditions of that song ever and *Blue Bayou* by Roy Orbison is one of the best songs ever written. I talk about a lot more things until the lights go off. I was finally able to sleep the next morning.

When I wake up, I can still vaguely remember what I thought about when I could not sleep. I realize that no one will ever get to see that. But anyway, it was a nice tool to get some sleep. I was once a Summer Guest. In my own bedroom, that is, and again when I cannot sleep tonight. I slide back in the studio. I had not yet finished my story.

JUST AS IN THE FILM

The sound of his phone is turned off and the 3D glasses stands on his nose. There is yet another film to the point of beginning. The light goes out and the mysterious music leads the nearly two-hour film. It's a superhero movie. The man in the movie goes against the scum who took the absolute power on earth. There's also that beautiful woman. He loves this kind of movies. So unrealistic, but who cares. This is finally his moment. It is a moment where he can leave reality behind. His life wasn't so bad. He has a job. Many people love him. He regularly praises with happy life he has. But today, he is just seeking anonymity in the cinema.

He has a vivid imagination and would just love to save the world from its demise. But I wish he would begin closer to home and save his own world first. Unfortunately, he does not realize that it's not all about being heroic by beating aliens. The film is just his kind of salvation. In real life, he is facing some major challenges. His girlfriend loves him, but he was reluctant about her. She lets him know, all the time, that she's ready for the next step, but he's just not convinced that he feels the same. There's a certain fear in him: fear of losing what he has carefully built for all these years. For now, she is beinh patient, but for how long?

She realizes that he just has to get used to sharing his life with her. He is still learning to settle. She knows he doesn't want to lose her, but sometimes, it's as if he is in deep abyss; he doesn't know what to do. If it were all up to her, she already would have to take the plunge.

The film has ended and he is staring at the white screen. He just realized a couple of things. He has to get out of his world; the world in where almost everything has a good outcome; the world wherein the good always prevails, and if not, there would always be a sequel where it will end the way he wants it. He knew that world too well. Now is the time to make decisions for his own life. He will go to her and be a hero. He will tell her that he wants a life with her; that he wants to build a future with her. No more waffling because he had done that long enough.

The lights in the theatre go on again. It was time to go; time to start to work on his superhero role. It was time to take action. Just like in the movie, but without the violence. Just like in the movie, but without the mask. Just like in the movie, with his heart and his own new world.

WISH

It's crowded in the city. Many people have found their way outside to enjoy the summer sun. He is one of them. On the bench, he looks at everyone walking by. He enjoys the diversity among all of them; the many differences that make them all unique anc pleasant. He sits for a little more time. Today is his day; he has time for himself.

It was about two years ago that he was here too. His life at that time looked very different. It was not better or worse; it was different. It was too easy for him to give judgments to the quality of life, back then. Now, he had a lot of wishes which he really hoped to come true. The path, which he followed back then, was interesting, but he also felt like there was a sword hanging just above his head all the time. Luckily, everything went according to plan. Thinking back to that chapter of his life made him glad that it was all over.

While he thinks he sees young people in groups with backpacks walking by. They were probably the students who can't resist the need to work. For now, he could not bear to think about that.

When he was young, he worked hard for his driver's license, and finally getting it was quite an achievement during that time. It had been a good few years, but major setbacks did occur. He was disappointed in love for several times but that's part of being young. He strongly believed that that will never happen again. All in all, he was a happy man in the middle of the crowd. Many of his dreams have come true. He had managed to get a nice apartment, and he had many hobbies.

He realized that there was still much to be desired, but now, there were limits to what was possible even though he had the feeling that he was on top of the world. He had the confidence to grow. But the feeling of receiving the applause of a packed house after a play, opening his own exhibition of paintings, and having a wedding ring slid in his finger as a sign of great love were the moments that he would love to experience. Would they ever happen?

The future never lays its cards on the table. He would have to contribute himself and that was his intention. But on the other hand, he liked to dream. It gave him hope. It made him have a lot to look forward to, no matter how bizarre his dreams were.

He stood up and went into the crowd. A Chinese philosopher once said that freedom from desires would give inner peace and real joy in life. That thought gave him a good feeling. The thirst he had would be quenched soon and that idea made him feel better.

THOSE WHO KNOW FOR SURE

In America, lives a certain community. They are not very popular in their country. They are part of the *Westboro Baptist Church*.

I had never heard of this community, until I saw a documentary about them. What I saw was that they said they had a clear opinion on many issues, and that was made clear in a certain way. The community holds demonstrations at various places in the country. One of the reasons why they preach is homosexuality. It is said that homosexuality (or any other "violation of law") is a form of insult to God. Through various scriptures, they try to substantiate this. Many things are considered as sin, and they are happy when people are punished for their sins. When someone dies in a traffic accident, for them that is something to be happy about. It was the wrath of God that made it happen. When a soldier died in the war, the news was received with joy. God has his reasons for that to happen.

They are extremists in my eyes. Although they don't use violence, their thoughts are, in my eyes, so extreme that they have lost their humanity. Their indoctrination has made them hateful beings. The void can be read in their eyes.

A reporter once asked one of them if what his thought was about when one of his kids who ran away because she could not tolerate such views of her parents. He and his wife seem to not mind. They believe that if she does not want to conform to the ideology that is taught to them, then they are glad that she ran away. That is both sad and shameful to see.

I have been friends with people who lived in the Bible belt. Although they were not as extreme in their actions as the community in America, they still had similarities. They believed in a moody and vengeful God. They believed that man is not in control of his own fate, but it's in the hand on God. When the subject of belief was raised, it was like I ran into a wall.

Everything they thought, they knew for sure. What's written is what it is. Every other option was simply unthinkable. Everything won't be difficult when you leave it all to God. It was their truth; their only truth, so there's no reason to seek for other truths. Those who believe, do not allow themselves to be inspired by people who have different opinions. The way I see it, it's impossible to influence them. It's like they always have their fingers in their ears while singing.

FREE

In my teenage years, I bought my first walkman. It was a small black box with buttons.

It needed four batteries. The Walkman was, in fact, fond of batteries. After a few hours of play, the music starts to slow down. It's quite a bit of my own fault. I often pressed the "fast forward" and "rewind" button. Not that I'm complaining. I liked it a lot that I could take my favorite music anywhere with me.

Over the years, the Walkmans got smaller, more compact, and they had less and lesser need for batteries. I still used them when I went on the road. Music is an important part of my life and I want to be able to enjoy it wherever I am. But at one point, I noticed that it had become an issue. I just wasn't able to survive without it. I had to have it everywhere with me, and if not, I just really miss it.

The transition from the walkman to an mp3 player didn't go well for me. I wasn't really good with technology. I gave up on it and I just sat down in silence. It turned out that I liked it.

If there was no music in my ears, I had a lot more space in mind, and that causes me to think more. The absence of music made me feel more comfortable. I became much more aware of my state of mind. I gave my mind the attention it deserved. But in the end, I wasn't able to resist music. I bought another mp3 player, then I was back to where I always was.

While I'm writing this, I have a phone on my other hand, and an mp3 on the other. The phone occupied a prominent place in my life. Now, I start to think that it's too prominent. I don't think it's true that it intended to make lives easier. I think it's intended to take over lives, and keep it in power. Am I happy with my phone? Certainly. Is it useful? Absolutely. But can we live without everything that wee see on it from the social media? Yes, we can!

In a sense, the phone is quite an extra baggage. It pressures us to read messages from other people. And let's face it: the majority of those messages are not important enough for us to be reading. Someone is out for dinner tonight? Fun. It's almost the weekend? I know, I know. It's snowing outside? I know because I have my own windows. Why do I read all that nonsense? Even worse, why do I do it too? I have always been in control of what I do and when I do it. Such phone should not be able to decide for me. If only it was easy to get rid of it. I don't even remember the last time I put it down, and had a sense of freedom.

BUILDING BRIDGES

When feud threatens peace between people, we retreat to our island to sit with self-pity. The distance between people seems bigger than ever. Between one island and another appears to be an unbridgeable ocean that is restless and accessible by the raging storm. Everyone has their own side of the story.

Pride is a good because it gives us a sense of self. But pride can also get in the way. Then there's arrogance. We are high on our throne, and we refuse to admit that.

When one admits to being wrong, it is seen differently. Being the first one to step down and apologize could be taken as a sign of weakness. And because we have pride, we do not want to take that risk.

Being able to let go of that pride, and to admit our own mistakes, provide the materials to complete the bridge. We need willingness to build that bridge in order to obtain harmony.

The realization that certain behaviors have different reasons also contributes to understanding. You do not have always had to agree, but you could always try to understand the situation. It takes, perhaps, a little bit of malice to be able to put a few boards back on that bridge towards the other person. Just a little more understanding; a little more willingness to look. Nothing is what it seems and all behavior comes from somewhere. No human is alien to us, after all. We are similar in many aspects even though we don't always realize that. The emotions of the other are in everyone. One just dispenses them in a different way than the other.

Also, anger is a part of who we are. If only we, at some point, have the will to straighten things out, and listen to the story of the other. No matter how much we think that the law is on our side, there is still the other side of the table. We all have our side of the story and everyone wants to heard and recognized. If we all start to listen, we all might meet halfway across the ocean and the distance would be less than expected.

LESS IS MORE

Some time ago, there was a debate about Islam. Muslims were on one side of the table. Ex-Muslims/critics on the other side. The proposition was: Islam is a religion of peace. Of course everyone had an opinion on this subject and there were also firm discussions, but all of that hardly ever came close to each other. Let alone that eventually a single answer to the argument could be given. There was just too much to say about it. The interpretations of that faith were too diverse. Items from the news were cited by critics to support their right. Quranic verses were used to speak against each other. I saw it all and it made me dizzy. After the debate, I took the time to find out what my real opinion is on that matter. I was just ready to ponder. It took me some time. Is Islam a religion of peace? I don't really think I can answer that. I am not a Muslim, but that doesn't mean I don't have a thing for that religion.

Firstly, I wonder if there is such a thing as Islam as a whole. As with Christianity, there are many currents. And those currents have ramifications. So many people, so many opinions.

It is therefore, ultimately, the people who are contributing to a religion. A religion without followers is only a shell practice. It was made by people working on it everyday to be inspired by Islam. It is the people who put their lives in service of Islam, and practice different opinions. There are about twenty different currents within Islam. In many ways, they have similarities but did the sacred book have been clear and obvious why there are so many sub-currents? Precisely because the book provides plenty of room for interpretation, people can start off with different truths. "It's like a timetable." said Fons Jansen once. Define your end and you'll always be there. Take a stand and a text will support the same. It is both good news for both the secular and the extremists. There is no consensus, no connection which leads to an explanation. ***** Islam as a whole does not exist. It is too diverse.

Then there are the five pillars of Islam: The profession of faith, the ritual prayers, almsgiving, fasting and pilgrimage to Mecca. I regularly visit forums on the Internet for Muslim youth. I wonder how the five pillars are still significant to them. It looks like as if other values have always been there. One reads another lesson about what you should do as a Muslim. I read one rarely urging each other to pray for world peace and introspection. Other values seem to have taken place in some Muslims.

Through the maze of various rules, the core sometimes seems to be lost. Many young Muslims are still looking for clarity within all rules.

I know, these adolescents are not only representative of a religion. On the other hand, I wonder why there is no mention of love and friendship into the five pillars. Why is the recognition on a man who lived 1400 years ago, and not on the helping hand you can reach out to a stranger? Why is making the pilgrimage up the acquisition of knowledge about other religions? There is still a lot I do not understand, and maybe I will also never understand. The more I learn, the more questions arise. I plead for a simplification of Islam because of the Muslims themselves.

The ultimate goal should be having unity among the people; them, not drowning in rules, commandments, and prohibitions so one does not feel guilty about asking critical questions, since, apparently, Islam tolerates no contradiction in its "moral authority."

The simplification is: do knowledge, treat others as you want to be yourself, and treat them in good terms. Help the poor and the weak, and be content with little. Make statements that give room for interpretation. But still, some of the chapters of Quran can be interpreted the way they shouldn't be.

I had been happy to present in the debate about Islam, not to pick on others, but to gain knowledge. Because religious or not, in the end, I am convinced that we are all better off to understand one another. If I were starting a new religion, that would be one of the first commandments. Not that I would have many supporters. People would find those commandments to simple. People would rather be divine.

A BEAUTIFUL DAY

There was that one year that is not exactly an easy year. It seemed like all of the jerks and bitches in the world are stuck in one room, and I sat there, with them. It was the sad reality in which I was trapped.

In general, I have always been in great classes. From kindergarten to the college years, I've almost always had a good time. There was a sense of belonging that has only grown stronger over the course of the year. But now, things were different. I was on the early years of my high school, and I was on my puberty stage. Mopeds, smoking, clothing and music were not to be underestimated parts of everyday life. A lot of my classmates were so interested in those things but I was not. A lot of things didn't matter to me. I didn't care what brand of shoes you wore. It didn't matter if you had moped, and somehow, because of that, I was not exactly the most popular person in class.

As mentioned, the classroom was filled with people I did not like. They were just very annoying. They were frequently sent to detention for talking back to the teacher, or starting fights in the schoolyard. Classes, at that time, were not so great. And then there were the girls. They were not much better. Most of them were arrogant and those who were not, was because they didn't allow themselves to be carried away. All in all, it was no fun to be in school. There were still people whom I interacted with, but they could not compensate for that miserable school. I was regularly harassed because, apparently, I was an outsider. In my memory, it was always cloudy in that school. There's no sunshine in my memory that was etched from that time.

The teachers were also not happy. I have seen many of them lose self-control. It worked, but no one really listened to what they were saying. Everyone would be silent for about five minutes. At one time, a teacher was so tired that he hit his fist on the table, and the whole class almost had a heart attack. "I want to fuck you to be quiet!" he bellowed.

I failed that year. It was not so bad because I went to a different school. I got the chance to develop myself in a positive way. I have never seen those pesky people from that school again, like this one kid. I don't remember his name. He would always tease me, and I was just stupid in his eyes for not doing what all of them did. I haven't seen him until after I graduated college. I saw him bored standing and leaning against a fence. He looked a bit shabby. Of course he made me remember that school. He was one of the popular ones at that time. I could not help but to smile from within. The train arrived exactly on time that day. The sun was shining. I had a degree in. In many ways, it was a beautiful day.

THE GLASS WALL

One of my biggest fears is stationary; to standstill; to not be able to move forward; to remain in a place where I ended long ago. It really does not matter what place it is. It is not because the place is creepy; it's having the idea of not getting any further.

I wonder where the idea came from. Why do you always want more than what you have already achieved? Where did the idea of never having enough came from? How did we know that there is always more? Is that cultural, in my DNA, or something that I have taught myself?

I imagine a world behind a glass wall to see it all; how the world is changing around my back; how people get older, change jobs, get to know other people, and get married again. I see it all happen, and in the meantime, I stand where I am. There is something sad from being trapped behind the wall while everyone else is living their lives.

Perhaps the fear of getting caught goes hand in hand with the failure to achieve dreams. How could you go with life without having ambitions no matter how big or small they are in the eyes of others? You need dreams to chase and that is human nature. You could be the predator in order to stay alive.

But really, one of my biggest fears is stationary; seeing opportunities but not being able to grab any of it because of the glass wall that separates you from the real world. Perhaps the glass wall is a symbol of loneliness; not having the ability to connect with other people. That's arrest, in a sense; having no relationships that you can develop, and having no people around whom you can learn from or mean something to.

I have encountered glass walls in my path. Those were during the times when I wasn't sure of what I really wanted. Those were emotional moments, and all I could do was to cherish what I had. I've learned to just be with what I have, to enjoy the little things in life, and to be happy for others. Being happy helps push the glass wall away, and it just means that I'm never completely silent.

THE PATH AND THE GOAL

"Not the goal is important, but the road to it." I once heard someone say. To me they are both equally important. I want to achieve my goals and taking the path should be pleasant as much as possible. I do realize that some roads are full of potholes, but I also realize that sometimes I can take a big detour to get anywhere that is no different. I take that for granted. It's never quite as you expected. The expectation is never equal to what it really is when you get there.

It was a long time ago. I was sitting in a car at The Hague. The man in front of me asked me what I was now doing. He was not whining. He was just watching me drive because he knew that I could do it. I had been working for years to get my license, and every time I took the test, something would go wrong so I get declined. After five times of trying and failing, the CBR had had it with me. They sent me to Rijkswaterstaat. I felt very small during that time.

I've had three different driving instructors at two different schools. I paid for a lot of classes and dry runs, but all of that didn't work. Driving exams were like games that I just couldn't win. That was what I always thought about when I get in the car. It all went wrong when I'm pulling away. I wasn't able to see the cyclist and almost hit him. That was the first incident, but I could start all over again.

"And now we really start" the man said. I got my act together. Once we were on the road and slid past the time, I got more and more confident. My most dreaded part, entering the highway, went easy. The highway had just been constructed and the cars were to be counted on one hand. Everything went really well. But sometimes, we do things that we cannot explain afterwards, except by saying how stupid it was.

We are waiting for a traffic light. The man asks me whether I am interested in Formula 1 sport. As far as I know, it had nothing to do with my driving style. I told him my heart is more in football. The light turns green. I turn the steering wheel to the left. I talk about my expectations about the upcoming match of the Dutch national team. At that moment, I hear "What are you doing?" The man next to me was then, giving a tug on the steering wheel to avoid the oncoming traffic punctures. I got carried away with our good conversation. When we got back, I park the car and walk on his instructions to the building. We sit down and brace myself to hear the bad news; To I hear that I'm a jerk. But I hear him say that I can drive very well but it just does not show. He give me more speech and I felt like a suspect on a hearing. The verdict: "I'll let you go on one condition: You're going to ride well because i know you can. You're a free man. The pink paper is yours."

"Not the goal is important, but the road to it." I was glad that I had finally reached the damn goal.

SELFISH

It may sound selfish, but in my life I am the most important thing there is. There are many lovely people around me. I would not want to lose them. I love them very much, and I'm finally at the center of all these people. This idea is less radical than it might seem. I can be the happiness of someone else. Delighted, I give everyone the best but at the end of the song, it's all about my own happiness. The interpretation I give to their creation is not universal; everyone is different. In my daily life, I try not to focus on just myself, and in that way, I try to pursue happiness.

Your own satisfaction is always the goal. The poet Christopher Morley said that there is only one success: Live your life in your own way, and happiness will flow continuously. Over the years, I gradually learned what is good for me. I surround myself with people I like. I develop interests and do things with them. I set goals for myself and try to achieve them.

To achieve all this, I need other people. Without others, there is a big part of my happiness taken away. I try to enjoy the little things that life offers. Whatever people are satisfied with, I won't make it worse or even better. Money is relative. If I am not satisfied with myself, then no amount of money can compensate.

Therefore, I am glad I finally know what makes me happy. I just love to be able to have a day for myself. It gives me the opportunity to think about myself, about what I want to do, and who I am. It works best when I'm alone.

It might sound selfish, but in my life I am the most important thing there is. If I'm good for myself, I can also be good to others. And that is not being selfish.

BROTHERLY LOVE

Small as he was, he walked with quick steps behind his big brother. He had no choice. The beach was crowded and to not get lost, he followed the trail of the person who would know how to return to the place where the towels were. You can always count on big brothers. They know the way. You just need to follow the steps and then all will be well. The little boy had an attitude of "where you go, I go." And that was the best choice he could make at that time. The beach was full. The weather was warm. The sea was exciting but now it was time to return home. Wherever he goes, the little boy would go. He put all his hopes and trusts in his big brother because that will make everything okay.

Many years later, they sat facing each other. Much had already happened. The little boy had learned to find his own way. He was no longer small. The road to becoming an adult was accompanied by trial and error. The big brother was often there for him to listen to the stories he told about the whole process; the doubts, the joys, the sorrows and the new start that was always there. The big brother recognized all these feelings, because he had been there. The story of the boy, who was once small, sounded strange to the big brother's ears. It was no longer, "where you go, I go." But their trust in each other was still there. Wherever they go, they would always meet again. Always and everywhere. Just like when they were the little boys on the beach, but now as adult men in life.

THE WALK

We have been together for so many years. We walked over bridges, past ponds, through parks, streets and squares and beaches. We had our regular routes. We sat on benches, enjoying the people walking by and the sunlight that warmed us. We walked so often that we don't remember it all. The walks were never boring. We talked about life and what kept us busy. There have been times when I wondered how many steps were still ahead of us.

Not that there are problems lurking, but I knew from experience that what you have today, can be history by tomorrow. My life was subject to change. I knew I did not want to let this pass, but I always had uncertainties. Looking back, I've never had certainties.

The walk we started together will not always be easy. The sunlight would be there but sometimes, the rain would make the parks where we love to come, look lost and lonely. The bridges that bring us to the other side, would they always be there to patiently wait for us?

I remember when we were walking on a trail. The twilight had begun but the low sun cast light for us. A walk with you gives no guarantees for the future, but it always gives us hope for what is yet to come.

Printed by BoD™in Norderstedt, Germany